POPPY'S CHAIR

by Karen Hesse • *illustrated by* Kay Life

Macmillan Publishing Company   New York
Maxwell Macmillan Canada   Toronto
Maxwell Macmillan International   New York   Oxford   Singapore   Sydney

Text copyright © 1993 by Karen Hesse. Illustrations copyright © 1993 by Kay Life.
All rights reserved. No part of this book may be reproduced or transmitted in any form or by any means, electronic or mechanical, including photocopying, recording, or by any information storage and retrieval system, without permission in writing from the Publisher. Macmillan Publishing Company is part of the Maxwell Communication Group of Companies. Macmillan Publishing Company, 866 Third Avenue, New York, NY 10022. Maxwell Macmillan Canada, Inc., 1200 Eglinton Avenue East, Suite 200, Don Mills, Ontario M3C 3N1.
First edition. Printed in the United States of America. The text of this book is set in 14 pt. Bembo. The illustrations are rendered in pastel.

1   3   5   7   9   10   8   6   4   2

Library of Congress Cataloging-in-Publication Data. Hesse, Karen. Poppy's chair / by Karen Hesse ; illustrated by Kay Life.   p.   cm. Summary: On her first summer visit to her grandmother since her grandfather's death, Leah is saddened by his absence, but Gramm helps her learn how to remember Poppy with joy. ISBN 0-02-743705-1 [1. Death—Fiction. 2. Grandfathers—Fiction. 3. Grandmothers— Fiction.] I. Life, Kay, ill. II. Title. PZ7.H4364Po 1993   [E]—dc20   91-47708

In loving memory of my mother-in-law, Vera, and my grandmother, Sara
In loving celebration of my mom, Franny
—K. H.

To Poppy's grandchildren
—K. L.

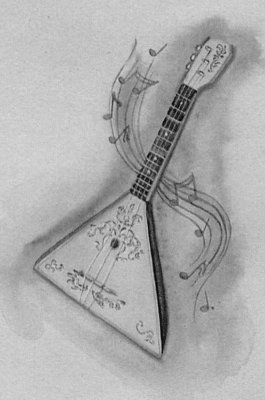

Every summer Leah spends two weeks with her grandparents, Gramm and Poppy. But this summer is different. This summer, when Leah is dropped off, only Gramm is waiting on the back porch.

The next morning, Leah and Gramn get ready for a day of shopping. Leah slips into her white dress with pink ribbons in the sleeves.

Poppy smiles at Leah and Gramm from the picture on the night table, but Leah tries not to look at it. Leah is afraid of Poppy's picture.

While Gramm is dressing, Leah sorts through Gramm's jewelry box. She sits on the edge of Gramm's bed and untangles a bracelet with big yellow stones.

"Would you like to wear that today, Leah?" Gramm asks.

Carefully, Leah puts the yellow bracelet back in the box. "I'm wearing my charm bracelet, Gramm," she says, holding up her arm.

Gramm pulls on her girdle and stockings in front of the mirror. She puts on a flowered dress and clips on earrings. Her hat and pocketbook and shoes all match.

Gramm brushes rouge across Leah's cheeks and touches Really Red lipstick to Leah's lips. Leah smudges her lips together to make the lipstick spread, just the way Gramm does. They look at their faces side by side in the mirror.

"Time to catch the bus," Gramm says.

Leah and Gramm never took the bus before. Poppy always drove them in his big green Ford.

The bus smells like old shoes, but Gramm, squeezed against Leah on the hard seat, smells like roses. Gramm's neighbor, Mrs. Goldfarb, settles into a seat across the aisle. She takes a picture from her purse and passes it to Gramm. "Look what I found yesterday."

Gramm holds the photo. "Look, Leah," she says. "It's Poppy."

Leah turns away from the picture of Poppy planting flowers in the backyard. She looks at Gramm's face. Gramm's eyes are so sad.

Leah scowls at Mrs. Goldfarb while Gramm tucks the photo into her purse.

Leah and Gramm stay all day at Ingleside Mall and come home with three bags and a bakery box. "What bargains we got," Gramm says, spreading out a new pair of stockings, three dish towels, and matching flowered dresses. "But I wish we could have found a new charm for your bracelet, Leah."

"Picking out charms was Poppy's job," Leah says.

Gramm makes kasha with bow tie noodles for dinner. Leah snitches a bow tie from the heavy iron pot, the way she and Poppy always did. Gramm pretends not to notice.

Leah and Gramm save the chocolate-top cookies from Silber's bakery for dessert. Leah cuts the string around the bakery box and sticks her nose inside, breathing in the sugary smell.

"Mmmm," she says. "My stomach feels like a big hole."

"Even with all those bow ties you ate?" Gramm asks.

Leah nods.

While Gramm washes dishes, Leah dries.

"Sing the song about the balalaika," Gramm says.

Leah loves that song. It's a riddle song from Russia, played on a funny, triangle-shaped guitar. Leah taught the song to Poppy a long time ago.

"I don't want to sing it now, Gramm."

Leah tries to keep the song out of her mind as she wipes and stacks the dishes. It comes back to her, anyway.

Tumbala, tumbala, tumbalalaika,
Tumbala, tumbala, tumbalalaika.

Leah pushes the new dish towel through the handle of the silverware drawer, where it hangs to dry.

Leah and Gramm go upstairs, and Gramm fills the tub.

"I'll just take off this girdle," Gramm says. "You'll meet me downstairs when you finish, Leah?"

Leah nods. When she is alone in the tub, the balalaika song keeps running through her mind.

Tumbala, tumbala, tumbalalaika

Leah rushes through her bath and joins Gramm downstairs in the living room.

"You want to watch television?" Gramm asks.

Leah nods and goes over to the cabinet with the television set inside. The clasp makes a ringing sound as Leah tugs open the doors.

Gramm and Leah curl up on the silky sofa, Gramm in her flowered housecoat and Leah in her pajamas. Neither of them sits in Poppy's chair. Leah hasn't gone near Poppy's chair since he died.

At bedtime, Gramm walks Leah upstairs. "Will you be all right until I come up?" Gramm asks.

Leah nods slowly.

"Would you like to sleep in my bed?"

Poppy used to sleep in that bed, and his picture is there. "No, thank you," Leah says.

So Gramm tucks Leah into Mom's old bed and turns out the
light. Leah watches the car shadows climb the wall and trail
across the ceiling and disappear. In the dark, she touches the
charms on her bracelet, naming each one. "Unicorn, teddy bear,
ballerina, rocking chair…"

Leah holds the charms and remembers Poppy, his soft hands,
his smoky voice. She thinks about Gramm's eyes, so sad on
the bus.

Suddenly Leah wants Gramm. She runs into Gramm's room, but Gramm's bed is empty. Only Poppy's picture is there, on the night table, smiling at Leah.

Leah bolts from Gramm's bedroom. She feels the stiff carpet under her bare feet as she rushes down the stairs. Gramm isn't on the silky sofa. Gramm isn't in the kitchen. Gramm isn't anywhere.

Leah runs back to the living room again.

Gramm *is* there, in Poppy's chair, wearing her flowered housecoat, her stockings rolled down around her ankles.

"Gramm! Gramm!" Leah cries.

Gramm opens her eyes, blinking at Leah from Poppy's chair. "What is it, Leah?" Gramm asks.

"Gramm, I couldn't find you," Leah says. "And then I did find you and you were in Poppy's chair and—Gramm, I don't want you to die!"

Gramm opens her arms, welcoming Leah into the big chair. Leah hesitates, then climbs onto Gramm's lap.

Gramm takes a deep breath. "When Poppy died, I felt terrible, Leah."

Leah touches the soft skin on the back of Gramm's hand.

"I wished Poppy could come back," Gramm says. "Sometimes I was even mad at him for dying."

Leah looks up at Gramm in surprise.

Gramm says, "I worried about what would happen to me. But you know what, Leah? Even though Poppy is gone, I'm all right."

Gramm strokes Leah's hair.

"And you know what else? I plan on living a long life. A life where every summer my granddaughter snitches bow ties from the pot while I pretend I'm not looking."

Leah smiles.

"A life where I can shop all day. And eat an entire box of chocolate-top cookies if I want."

Leah giggles.

"But, Leah," Gramm says, "someday I *will* die—"

Leah turns away.

"When I do, Leah, you're going to feel awful at first, just like you do now, about Poppy."

Gramm takes Leah's chin in her soft hands. "But sooner or later, you'll let those awful feelings go. Then you'll have room for the good feelings to come back again."

Leah looks at her bracelet with the charms dancing around her wrist. Each charm brings back a different memory of Poppy—and now each of those memories makes a good feeling inside Leah.

Leah snuggles closer to Gramm in Poppy's chair. She wraps her arms around Gramm and buries her head in Gramm's neck. Gramm smells like roses.

"Teach me your song about the balalaika," Gramm says, "so I can sing it myself when you're not here."

Leah and Gramm sit in the big chair and practice the song.

Tumbala, tumbala, tumbalalaika,
Tumbala, tumbala, tumbalalaika.

"Gramm," Leah asks as they climb the stairs, "when we go to Ingleside again, can we get a balalaika for my charm bracelet?"

Gramm ruffles Leah's hair. "We can try," she says.

"And can I sleep in your bed tonight?"

Gramm nods.

Leah gazes at the picture on the night table. She touches
Poppy's face.

"Could I have the picture from Mrs. Goldfarb?" Leah asks.
"The one of Poppy planting flowers."

"Of course," Gramm says.

Leah climbs into Gramm's bed. She remembers the mornings
when she'd snuggle between Gramm and Poppy and the silly
stories Poppy would tell her.

Then Gramm gets into bed and curls up beside Leah. Her soft body makes the bed warm and cozy.

"Goodnight, Leah," Gramm says.

"Goodnight, Gramm."

"Goodnight, Morris," Gramm says to the picture on the night table.

"Goodnight, Poppy," Leah says.

Leah wriggles around in Gramm's bed until she finds the perfect spot—halfway between Gramm's warmth and Poppy's smile.